Jake the Ballet DOG

Karen LeFrak
Illustrations by Marcin Baranski

WALKER & COMPANY
New York

"Wait for me, Jake," Allegra called to the little dog as he chased

snowflakes. She was watching him to help her friend Richie.

"Look at the Sugar Plum Fairy on the top of that tree," Allegra said.

Jake raised his head but spotted a toy mouse ornament instead.

He sprang for it with a hop, jump, and turn in the air.

"Bravo!" Allegra smiled. "You should be called Jake the *Ballet* Dog!

Tomorrow I'm going to take you to my dance class and *dress rehearsal* for

The Nutcracker ballet."

The next morning at the dance studio, Allegra introduced everyone to Jake. A young ballerina came over and stroked Jake's head and ears and under his chin.

"Jake, this is Anna," said Allegra. "In the ballet, she dances the role of Clara, who is given a Nutcracker soldier for Christmas and dreams all her toys come to life."

Jake widened his eyes at the word "toys."

"Who have we here?" asked Sergiev, the ballet master, when he entered the studio.

"This is Jake. He's going to watch and listen to our rehearsal. I promise he'll behave," Allegra said.

CLAP!
CLAP!

First

Second

Sergiev clapped his hands twice and gestured to the piano player to
begin. Jake watched the dancers warm up at the ballet *barre*. They
stretched their arms and legs and practiced bending their knees for *pliés*,

Third

Fourth

Fifth

using *five basic positions*. Now Jake assumed a doggie play position as he stretched *his* legs.

"Look at Jake," Anna said excitedly. "It looks like he's doing a *bow*!"

Ta-dah!

Allegra got her gym bag and pulled out a small toy. "That's not his only ballet step." Allegra smiled. "Watch this, everyone!" she said eagerly. Allegra tossed the toy softly across the room and—**WOOSH!**—Jake was off! With a majestic *tour en l'air*, like a *danseur noble*, he caught it before it could hit the floor. All the dancers applauded, no one louder than Anna. The pianist played two chords that sounded like "ta-dah!"

"I'll teach you some steps, Jake," said Anna. She shook the box of dog biscuits Allegra handed her. "Copy what I do and I'll give you a treat." Jake's ears stood up straight at the word "treat."

Jake watched Anna and, after a few flops, managed to perform a doggy *arabesque*.

Pirouettes made him dizzy.

But he was really good *en pointe*—he got on his tippy-paws to reach the biscuit Anna gave him.

Sergiev clapped his hands again and said, "Break time is over. It's time for

the dress rehearsal."

"We're going to put on costumes and makeup and come right back,"

Allegra said. "Stay on your special cushion and you can see the whole ballet

from here." Jake was about to snooze when he heard an *orchestra* with lots of violins playing. The violin was Jake's favorite instrument.

As the curtains opened, Jake saw an old-fashioned parlor with a Christmas tree. Anna, now dressed as Clara, and the other children were enjoying a holiday party.

Suddenly, the music
sounded mysterious. The lights
dimmed as a tall, thin man swirling a velvet
cape strutted onto the stage. Jake was on alert.

He growled and raced over to nip the stranger on his heels.

"Stop!" yelled Sergiev.

Anna stepped out of character and led Jake back to his cushion. She spoke to him calmly. "It's okay, boy. This is just a dancer playing Uncle Drosselmeyer. He's bringing us magical surprises!"

Jake sensed from her tone that nothing was wrong. **"Mmmmmmm."** He relaxed.

Errrrr...

When the rehearsal started again, Jake watched Clara whirl around, holding a new wooden Nutcracker soldier, her present from Drosselmeyer. But her brother, Fritz, tried to grab it. To Jake it looked like a game of tug-of-toy! He was about to join in when—**BAM!**—the Nutcracker fell and broke. Drosselmeyer bandaged it with his handkerchief and placed it in a doll's sleigh bed.

A peaceful melody signaled that the party was ending. Jake watched the guests leave and Clara and Fritz go off to bed. Just when he thought nothing else would happen, Jake saw Clara return in her nightgown. She cradled the Nutcracker in her arms and danced a solo, laid down on the sofa, and dozed off. Jake curled up on his cushion, too.

DONG, DONG, DONG. The grandfather clock chimed twelve and Clara's dream began to unfold on the stage. Jake watched as Drosselmeyer returned to work his magic. All at once, the lights flickered and Jake saw the Christmas tree grow taller and taller. Jake froze in amazement as some toys and ornaments came to life.

First one, then two, then twelve people-size mice crept toward Clara. Jake prepared to pounce on them, but—**POP!**—the harsh sound from a toy gun made him stop and quiver. "It might be thunder," he thought. Then, the Nutcracker and his soldiers charged into battle with the mice. Swords clashed. **CLINK, CLINK!**

Clara raised her slipper to hurl at the Mouse King. Wanting to protect her, Jake scurried to the nearest mouse, barking loudly. **"RUFF, RUFF!"** The mouse was so startled that it knocked into another mouse, who knocked into another mouse. Before Jake could bark again, all the mice tumbled to the ground!

As the *corps de ballet* howled with laughter, Jake ran around the toppled mice and took off with Clara's slipper.

Sergiev sighed. "Next scene, please."

Jake's eyes twinkled. Twirling among snowflakes were Clara and the

Nutcracker soldier, now turned into a handsome prince by Drosselmeyer.

Jake watched the prince place the Mouse King's crown, which had magically

become delicate and glittery, on Clara's head. As though she floated down

from the treetop, the Sugar Plum Fairy appeared and showed them to her

sleigh. Her diamond tiara caught Jake's eye. It was Allegra!

Luckily the curtain closed for a scenery change as Jake stood to greet her.
Anna went to settle him and explain what would happen next. "The Sugar
Plum Fairy is happy the mice are gone and has invited us to the Kingdom of
Treats."

"TREATS? Did she say, TREATS?" Jake seemed to say as he sat and offered
two paws, striking a begging pose.

When the music soared and the curtains reopened, Clara and her Nutcracker prince journeyed to an enchanted world and entered a candy castle that looked so real, Jake had to lick his chops.

The Sugar Plum Fairy waved her magic wand for delicious sweets to come alive and entertain them. Jake's tail wagged back and forth, back and forth, as Spanish Chocolates, Arabian Coffee, Chinese Tea, Russian Peppermints, French Bonbons, and Austrian Gingersnaps danced to special music from their foreign lands. Then, Candy Flowers waltzed with ever-so-graceful petals.

Before long, the Sugar Plum Fairy and a partner performed a *pas de deux*.
Like a real fairy, she hardly touched the ground. Jake arched his neck to
follow her as she was lifted high up. Then he lowered his gaze as she was
carefully returned to the floor.

A lullaby began and Drosselmeyer strolled by, one
last time. Everyone waved farewell, and Jake watched the
sleigh carry Clara and her prince home. Jake yawned.
The excitement of the ballet was making him sleepy.
While he rested, he noticed that the stage was changing
back into the parlor.

Clara was still asleep on the sofa, holding the mended Nutcracker. Jake
was certain her sofa was more comfortable than his cushion. And he wanted
another scratch and a snuggle, too. So, in a flash, he did the most energetic
chassé, *jeté*, *pas de bourrée*, whirl, twirl, and grand **PLOP**, right onto Clara's
lap. Clara popped up in surprise, and Jake covered her face with kisses.
Everyone, even Sergiev, laughed at the ballet's most unusual ending.

When it was time for Allegra to leave with Jake, Sergiev rubbed the pup's head affectionately. He leaned down and said to Jake, "You may come back for opening night, but only if you can stay OFFSTAGE."

"Don't worry," Allegra said cheerfully, "I have an idea."

On opening night, Allegra nodded to the dancer playing Drosselmeyer. He came forward with a present for Jake. Anna helped Jake open the box. One by one, Jake pulled out a furry family of toy mice and a large dog bone. Anna placed them all on his cushion.

"Ruff, ruff!" said Jake. First he licked Anna, then Drosselmeyer, then Allegra.

"These should keep him busy for a long time," said Anna.

"And in a pose of *repose*," added Allegra.

It worked! Jake stayed offstage for the entire ballet. The only mice he
nipped were his very own. At the final curtain call, Anna winked to Jake as
she took her most elegant bow. Then, with his nose peeking out from the
wings, Jake bowed, too.

FOOT NOTES

♪ **Arabesque:** A ballet step in which one arm and the opposite leg are held out straight

♪ **Ballet:** A story told only with music and dance. This is fine for Jake, who knows just a few words anyway, like "sit," sometimes "stay," and always "treat!"

♪ **Barre:** A handrail for dancers' warm-up exercises

♪ **Bow:** A ballet gesture at the end of class or a performance to show respect for the music and the art of dance

♪ **Chassé:** A ballet term meaning "to chase"

♪ **Corps de ballet:** A group of dancers who perform the same steps together, like the Snowflakes and Candy Flowers

♪ **Danseur noble:** An excellent male dancer, like Jake when he leaps in the air

♪ **Dress rehearsal:** A final practice, in costume, before the opening performance

♪ **En pointe:** Performing a ballet movement on one's toes

♪ **Five basic positions:** The basis for all other ballet steps

♪ **Jeté:** A ballet leap

♪ **The Nutcracker:** A ballet in two acts, based on a story by E. T. A. Hoffmann, for which Pyotr Ilich Tchaikovsky composed music more than one hundred years ago

♪ **Orchestra:** A group of musicians playing different instruments together. At the ballet, the orchestra is not onstage like at the Philharmonic. Instead, it plays from a pit in front of the stage. There are special instruments used for *The Nutcracker*, like the celesta with its tinkling bell sounds for the Sugar Plum Fairy

♪ ***Pas de bourrée:*** A combination of little ballet steps; in Jake's case, a *paw de bourrée*

♪ ***Pas de deux:*** A dance for two, like the famous Dance of the Sugar Plum Fairy with her partner

♪ ***Pirouette:*** A ballet spin

♪ ***Plié:*** A ballet step in which knees are bent and legs are turned out

♪ **Repose:** A still position, difficult for Jake to hold with so much activity going on

♪ ***Tour en l'air:*** A ballet turn in the air; one of Jake's special steps

♪ **Wings:** The sides of the stage from where Jake watches and listens—when he is not chasing strangers, mice, or tossed slippers

To "Jewel," whose *tour en l'air* and enchanting
bow could rival those of any prima ballerina
—K. L.

To my wife, Anna —M. B.

ACKNOWLEDGMENTS

To the following extraordinary people I present sugar
plums and pop-gun salutes: my literary agent, Fredrica
Friedman; publisher and editor Emily Easton; illustrator
Marcin Baranski; ballet consultants Sue Hogan and
Beverly D'Anne; dog fancier Thea Feldman; advisor T.
Byram Karasu; my husband, Richard LeFrak; and friends
Suzie and Richie Norton. To the adorable Jake, I give more
toy mice and dog treats than his cushion could hold.

New York City Ballet's production of George Balanchine's
The Nutcracker™ was the inspiration for the artist
in the creation of the artwork for the book.

George Balanchine's *The Nutcracker*™, choreography
by George Balanchine © The George Balanchine
Trust.

Text copyright © 2008 by Karen LeFrak
Illustrations copyright © 2008 by Marcin Baranski

First published in the United States of America in 2008 by
Walker Publishing Company, Inc.

For information about permission to reproduce selections from this book,
write to Permissions, Walker & Company, 175 Fifth Avenue, New York,
New York 10010

Library of Congress Cataloging-in-Publication Data
LeFrak, Karen.
Jake the ballet dog / Karen LeFrak ; illustrations by Marcin Baranski.
p.   cm.
Summary: Allegra takes her little dog Jake to ballet class for the rehearsal of
"The Nutcracker," and he proves himself to be a very good dancer.
ISBN-13: 978-0-8027-9658-5 • ISBN-10: 0-8027-9658-3 (hardcover)
ISBN-13: 978-0-8027-9659-2 • ISBN-10: 0-8027-9659-1 (reinforced)
[1. Dogs—Fiction. 2. Ballet dancing—Fiction. 3. Nutcracker (Choreographic
work)—Fiction.] I. Baranski, Marcin, ill. II. Title.
PZ7.L5211144Jak 2008   [E]—dc22   2007047653

Book design by Nicole Gastonguay
The artist used acrylic and tempera paint on Bristol paper to create the
illustrations for this book.

Visit Walker & Company's Web site at www.walkeryoungreaders.com

Printed in China
(hardcover) 10 9 8 7 6 5 4 3 2 1
(reinforced) 10 9 8 7 6 5 4 3 2 1